Licensed exclusively to Top That Publishing Ltd
Tide Mill Way, Woodbridge, Suffolk, IP12 1AP, UK
www.topthatpublishing.com
Copyright © 2016 Tide Mill Media
All rights reserved
0 2 4 6 8 9 7 5 3 1
Manufactured in China

Written by Oakley Graham
Illustrated by Olive May Green

ISBN 978-1-78445-772-3

A catalogue record for this book is available from the British Library

First day at SCHOOL

Illustrated by
Olive May Green

Written by
Oakley Graham

Panda, Fox and Donkey are the very best of friends!

It was the first day of school and they were all feeling a bit nervous.

The friends' nerves soon disappeared when they met their teacher, Miss Caribou. She had a smiling face and showed them where to hang their coats.

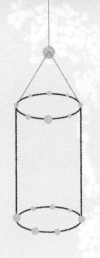

The first lesson was learning how to count. Donkey practised writing numbers and his new friend, Giraffe, stacked ten building blocks in the right order.

Then, Miss Caribou taught the class a song to remember the alphabet. Fox was good at remembering the letters and got a gold star for singing the alphabet in front of the class.

Everyone agreed that singing was a great way to learn the alphabet!

For the next lesson, the friends had to go to the school hall. Miss Caribou played the piano and the friends danced in time with the music.

Panda loved dancing, but Donkey was not so keen. He kept standing on his friends' feet!

Fox liked dancing too, but he enjoyed making different sounds on the musical instruments most of all.

After break, it was time for craft. Fox was scared that he would get messy, but Miss Caribou gave him an apron to keep his clothes clean.

Then the friends practised painting and using scissors. They worked together and made a giant collage to go on the classroom wall.

The collage was all the colours of the rainbow!

At 12 o'clock it was Donkey's favourite time of day – lunchtime!

Some children had lunch from the school canteen and others brought in a packed lunch from home.

After eating a healthy lunch, everyone had fun playing games with their new friends in the school playground.

After lunch, it was time for PE.

Mr Lion, the PE teacher, told the friends how important it is to stay active and exercise.

Everyone enjoyed running around the hall and climbing on the equipment, except Sloth. Poor Sloth was feeling poorly and could only sit and watch.

Story time was the last lesson of the day. Miss Caribou read the class an exciting story about travelling around the world. Then she listened to the older children read.

Donkey loved story time and was very pleased when he was given special word cards to practise at home.

Soon, it was time to go home. Panda, Fox and Donkey could not wait to continue their learning journey at school the next day.

SCHOOL
BUS
STOP